BEAUTIFUL YETTA

The Yiddish Chicken

By
DANIEL
PINKWATER

Illustrated by
JILL
PINKWATER

FEIWEL AND FRIENDS
NEW YORK, NY

It is night. A truck is driving on the highway. At the wheel is
Mr. Flegleman, the organic chicken rancher. In wooden crates are chickens.
The chickens are afraid. The truck rumbles through the darkness.

The truck pulls up in front of Phil's Poultry World, and with a tear in his eye,
Mr. Flegleman begins to unload the crates.

One of the crates has a loose lid. One of the chickens is brave and clever.
It is Yetta, beautiful Yetta. She sees her chance.
She struggles out of the crate and runs down the street.

Yetta, beautiful Yetta, will not be sold. She will not be soup.
She will not be roasted chicken on a Friday night. She is free.
She is in Brooklyn.

The streets of Brooklyn are strange to Yetta. Where is the grass?
Where are the flowers? It is not like Mr. Flegleman's chicken ranch.

There, Yetta and the other chickens led a happy life, running through the fields and eating bugs.

Oh, my beautiful home!

אוי, מיין שיינע היים!

oy, meyn SHAYneh haym!

Will you help me? I'm hungry.
קענסטו מיר העלפֿן? איך בין הונגעריק.
KENstu mir HELf'n? Ikh bin HOONgehrik.
Go back to the farm, silly hen!

Yetta wanders the streets of Brooklyn,
lonely, confused, unhappy.

What is this?
וואָס איז דאָס?
vos iz dos?

Then, Yetta sees a little green bird.
She has never seen a bird like it.

And, sneaking up behind the bird, sneakily, is a sneaky cat. The cat is getting ready to pounce.

Go away, you stinky cat!
גיי אַוועק, דו פֿאַרשטונקענע קאַץ!
gay ahVEK, du fahrSHTUNkehneh kahtz!

Yetta hears a voice above her head.

Look! That chicken saved Eduardo!
¡Miren allí! ¡Esa gallina salvó a Eduardo!
MEErehn aYEE! EHsa gahYINA sahlVO ah edWAHRdo!

Yetta looks up. Sitting on telephone wires are many little green birds.
They are parrots. Yes, parrots! There are flocks of wild parrots in Brooklyn.
Pet parrots flew away, found each other, had parrot babies,
and live very well in the streets and parks.

The chicken saved me. And look! Isn't she beautiful?

¡La gallina me salvó! ¡Y miren! ¿No es ella hermosa?

la gahYEEna me sahlVO! ee MEErehn, no ess EHya ehrMOsa?

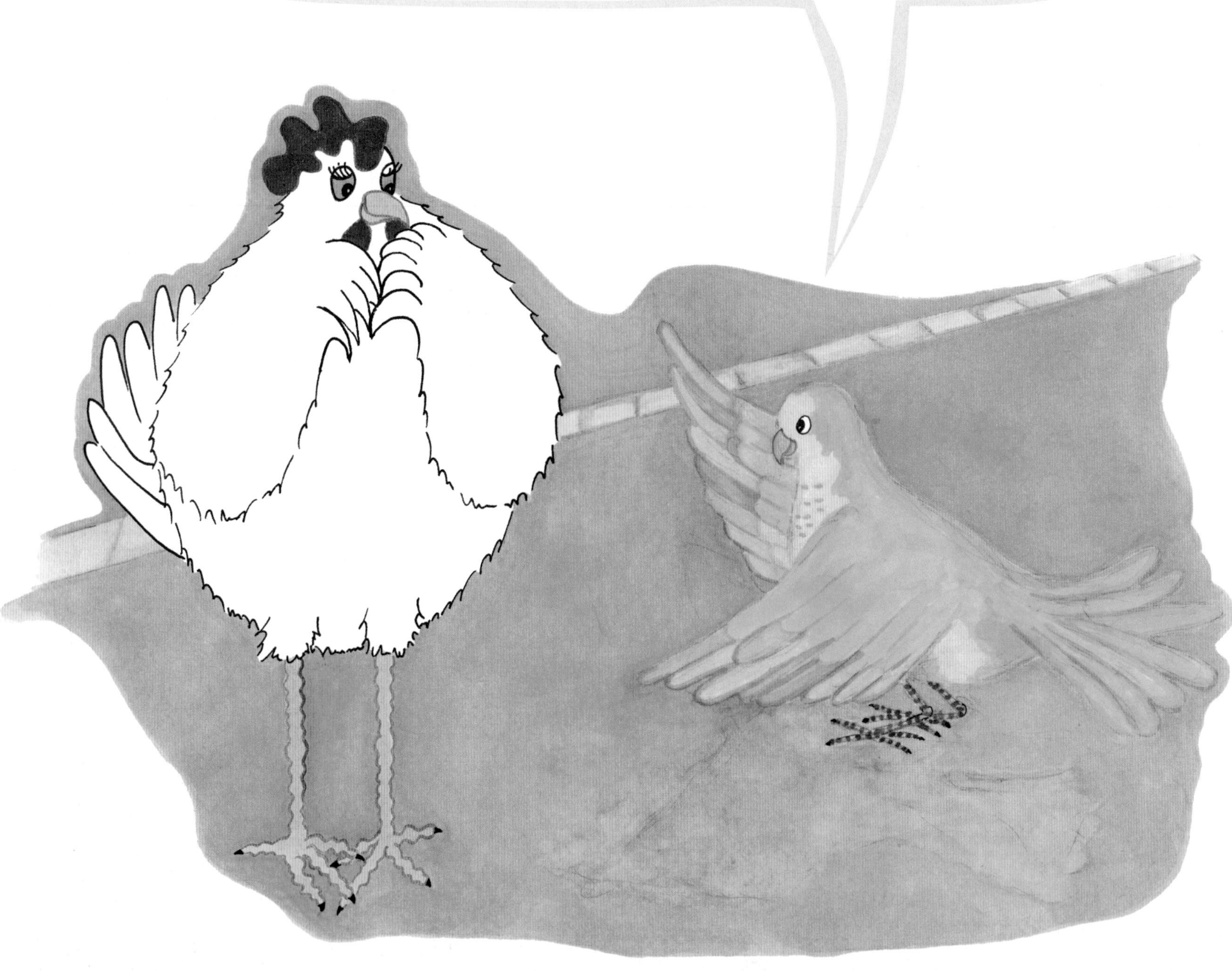

Come here, beautiful chicken. Sit with us!

¡Ven aquí, gallina hermosa! Siéntate con nosotros.

vehn aKEE, gahYEEna ehrMOsa! seeEHNtahteh con noSOtros.

I love this chicken.
Yo amo a esta gallina.
yo AHmo ah EHSta gahYEEna.

Please stay with us, beautiful chicken!
Por favor, quédate con nosotros, gallina hermosa.
pohr fahVOHR, KEHdahteh con noSOtros, gahYEEna ehrMOsa.

Yetta stayed with the wild parrots of Brooklyn.
They showed her how to find fruit and crusts of pizza.

And Yetta told them stories of her life in the country,

and chased cats away.

In time, because she was so beautiful, and because she could chase cats, Yetta became the leader of the parrots—or maybe their mother.

My dear children!
מײַן טײַערע קינדער!
meyn TEYehreh KINdehr

And they are still there—
you can go and see for yourself.

For Ed Weiss,
Physician, Yiddishist,
Chickenologist

A FEIWEL AND FRIENDS BOOK
An Imprint of Macmillan

Printed in March 2011 in China by Imago, Shenzhen. For information, address
Feiwel and Friends, 175 Fifth Avenue, New York, N.Y. 10010.

Library of Congress Cataloging-in-Publication Data Available

ISBN: 978-0-312-64441-3

Yiddish translation by Edward Weiss
Spanish translation by Guillermo Casallo

Book design by Barbara Grzeslo
Feiwel and Friends logo designed by Filomena Tuosto

First Edition: 2010

10 9 8 7 6 5 4 3 2

mackids.com

Yiddish and Hebrew use a different alphabet than English, and are written from right to left, instead of left to right (as in English). The chart to the right shows the Hebrew alphabet, written in Hebrew alphabetical order, so *Alef* is the first letter and *Tav* is the last. This alphabet is often called the "*aleph-bet*," because of its first two letters.

	Hebrew letter	Pronunciation	Letter name
	א	silent	Alef
	ב	B/V	Bet
	ג	G	Gimel
	ד	D	Dalet
	ה	H	He
	ו	V	Vav
	ז	Z	Zayin
	ח	Ch	Chet
	ט	T	Tet
	י	Y	Yod
	כ	K/Kh	Kaf
	ך	Kh	Khaf
	ל	L	Lamed
	מ	M	Mem
	ם	M	Mem
	נ	N	Nun
	ן	N	Nun
	ס	S	Samech
	ע	silent	Ayin
	פ	P/F	Peh
	ף	F	Feh
	צ	Ts	Tsadeh
	ץ	Ts	Tsadeh
	ק	Q	Qof
	ר	R	Resh
	ש	Sh/S	Shin
	ת	T	Tav